Monster In The Manor

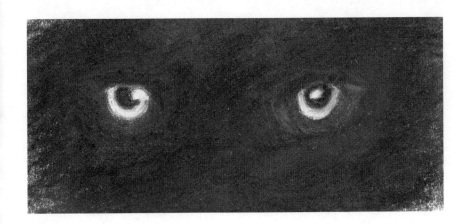

Ian Thomas

A monster living in an old manor?

Kids' personal belongings lost in an old manor?

What kind of monster is it?

Can a group of kids take on the monster and get their stuff back?

I would like to thank my Brother Nick for the drawing on my book cover, my Grandmother and her pets, my Dad for helping edit my book, my Mother for her encouragement. My Uncles, Aunts, and Cousins who support me. I would also like to thank Clay Ball and his wife Tabitha and their two daughters Savannah and Kasee, Katie Howland and her kids Noah and Emma, Kyle Jurek and his kids Ben and Allie, JD and Megan Morris and their kids Caroline, Braden, and Charlotte, Michael Morton and his family, Patrick Autry and his family, Amber Adams and her family, Sheryl Moriarty and her family, and all my friends who encourage me.

I would also like to thank my Grandfather, Fay Thomas, for surviving the war, for if he hadn't, I wouldn't be here and neither would my stories.

One day a group of kids were at the park playing soccer. They laughed, and they yelled "I'm open" and "I got it!" They were really having fun.

Suddenly the neighborhood bully comes and swipes their ball away. The kids tried to get the ball back from him, but he kept it high so they couldn't reach it. Then he runs off with it. The kids chased him.

The kids chased the bully across town. Suddenly, the bully stopped running. He turned to his left side and threw the soccer ball. When the kids saw where the bully threw it, they were shocked in terror.

The bully threw their ball into an old manor. The kids were too scared to go in there. Practically no one goes in there. It was believed that a monster lives in there. People have heard sounds, like growls, snarls and howls. Some say they've seen eyes and something hairy with teeth through the windows.

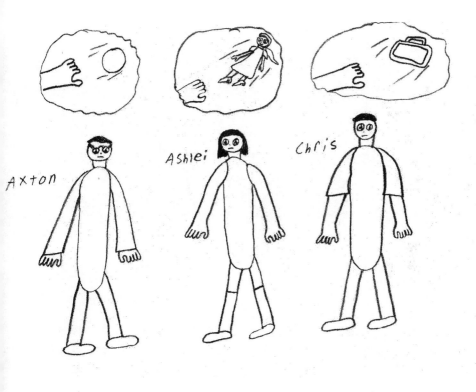

The kids Axton, Ashlei, and Chris were fed up with that bully. He's thrown their balls, toys, and even lunch boxes with lunch in them into the manor.

1(Axton)

This has gone far enough! It's time we take action.

2(Ashlei)

You said it, Axton.

3(Chris)

I have an idea.

Allie Ben Emma Noah

Chris' plan was to gather some of their friends, go into the manor, and get their stuff the bully threw in. So they got their friends Noah, Emma, Ben and Allie.

1(Ben)

Wouldn't it be easier if we just tell our parents?

2(Axton)

That's what I said.

3(Chris)

I don't think it will stop that bully from doing it again. Plus everyone is concerned about the monster. Besides, I always wanted to solve a mystery.

4(Emma)

The whole point of going in there is to get our stuff back; not hunt for monsters.

The kids went toward the front door. Chris turned the knob, and the door was unlocked. The kids went in, and they saw a paw print on the floor. It was definitely from an animal. The kids were wondering what kind of monster it was. Chris suggested they needed to split up. Axton was getting the feeling he was forgetting something.

Chris tells Noah to go with Allie, Axton to go with Ashlei, and Emma and Ben to come with him. Noah quietly says, "Yes!" Because he was searching with Allie. Axton just remembered what he forgot: He gets shy when he's alone with a girl, especially Ashlei.

Noah and Allie find what appears to be a den. They see a
bookshelf filled with books covered with dust, and a
couch that was as dusty as the books. The peculiar thing
they found was a fireplace with fire in it.

1(Noah)

Can a monster
make a fire?

2(Allie)

Not unless
this one
walks on
two feet.

3(Noah)

I suppose next you'll
tell me a person owns
the monster.

4(Allie)

Funny, I was thinking that.

Axton and Ashlei went upstairs. They walked down
a hallway. Axton saw a lot of rooms

1(Axton)

Why don't we split
up? You check the
rooms down there,
and I'll check these.

2(Ashlei)

I'm not going alone, and neither
are you. I don't want anything
bad happening to you.

Axton started to blush. They continued down the hall.

Chris, Ben, and Emma found the kitchen, and began searching in there. Ben took out a newspaper and told Chris and Emma it has a story about the manor.

1(Ben)

It says here that a man came in this place, and never came out. Everyone in town believes the monster ate him.

2(Chris)

I probably wouldn't say "everyone." And when exactly did you get that newspaper, Ben?

3(Emma)

He got it a month ago. I know because I got one too. Though I don't understand why he still holds on to it.

4(Ben)

To remind me why we should stay away from here, what else?

While searching in the kitchen, Chris was saying to Emma and Ben that he was surprised they didn't find any cobwebs. He walked through some and got caught in them, and yelled "Agh!" Emma and Ben laughed.

1(Emma)

You know, Chris, they do say to be careful what you ask for.

2(Chris)

Ugh! Who used to own this place, the Addam's Family?

3(Ben)

I probably would hav said "the Munsters." But that works, too.

Everyone was still searching for their stuff. Suddenly, Noah yelled. He yelled so loud the other kids could hear him. They were scared, because they didn't know who it was. They were afraid it might be the monster. Axton and Ashlei were so terrified they tripped and fell into one of the rooms.

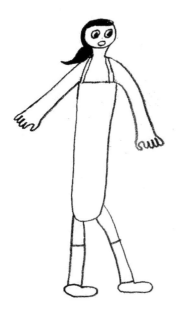 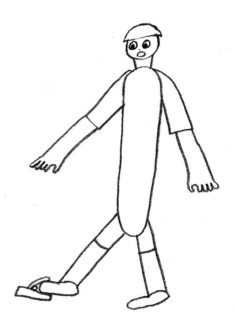

1(Allie)

Noah! What
happened?

2(Noah)

Something got
my foot!

3(Allie)

The monster!

4(Noah)

It's scary! It's
awful! It's, a
mousetrap?

5(Allie)

A mousetrap?
What's a set
mousetrap doing in
an old abandoned
manor?

6(Noah)

I don't
know, Allie.
But I have a
feeling we
will soon.

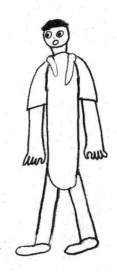

1(Chris)

Ben? Emma?
Did you two
hear that?

2(Ben)

I did.

3(Emma)

Yeah, so did I.

4(Chris)

Sounds like
someone is in
trouble.

5(Emma)

I almost
thought it was a
monster, but it
definitely
sounded like a
person.

6(Ben)

We better
go check to
see if our
friends are
ok.

1(Ashlei)

Axton? Do you suppose that was the monster?

2(Axton)

I don't think so, Ashlei. That sounded more like a yell than a roar.

3(Ashlei)

That may be one of our friends. We'd better go check on them.

4(Axton and Ashlei heard a hissing sound, and felt something warm.)

5(Ashlei)

Uhh, Axton? Was that you?

6(Axton)

I thought it was you.

Axton and Ashlei turned around, and saw eyes shining in the dark and sharp teeth. They yelled, "The Monster!" And ran out of the room, down the hall and back downstairs.

Axton and Ashlei met up with the others and told them they heard someone yell. Allie told them it was Noah and that he stepped in a mousetrap. Just before Axton and Ashlei could explain what they saw upstairs, the kids hear a snarling sound. They hear step sounds and see paws with sharp claws. The kids all yelled "Monster!" and ran into the other room.

The room they ran into was a dining room. Chris still had some of the cobweb he got tangled in. Axton took a look at it, and saw the web is not real, just part of a Halloween decoration. Everyone was surprised, and wondered what is with the web props and set mousetrap. Suddenly the lights turned on, and the kids gasped. Then they heard a voice say, "Can I help you kids?"

They turned around and saw a man. Ben took out his newspaper and saw, that he was the man who disappeared in the manor. The kids asked him who he was and what he was doing in an old abandoned building. The man introduced himself as Randy and told them the manor may be old, but it's not abandoned, and that it's his home.

1(The Kids)

Say what?

2(Ben)

Wait. What about the monster?

3(Randy)

Monster?

Suddenly they heard a sound. The kids saw they left the doors opened and saw the monster. The kids gasped and wondered what kind of monster it was. Could it be a behemoth? Could it be a werewolf? Could it be some kind of wild animal like a lion? Randy began to chuckle.

1(Randy)

Relax. It's just Brodie.

The kids were surprised that Randy said the monster's name was Brodie. Then it became a really big surprise because the monster turned out to be a dog. A rottweiler. Randy told the kids not to worry, and that he's really friendly. He was right, because Brodie walked up to the kids, and they petted him. The kids were thinking this has to be the friendliest monster they have ever seen.

Suddenly, Brodie started growling. The kids were wondering why. Randy said, "He's back." Then a football flies and breaks through one of the windows.

The kids asked Randy who he was talking about when he said, "He's back." He told them it was the neighborhood bully, and that he's been throwing stuff at his manor, and breaking his windows for a long time, and has not had a chance to take off some of the Halloween decorations.

1(Chris)

Well that explains the cobwebs.

2(Randy)

Yeah. Whenever Brodie smells him close by, he growls, because he knows that he is bad.

3(Allie)

Smart dog.

4(Ben)

That stuff is ours and other kids in the neighborhood. He's been taking our stuff and throwing them in here.

Randy told the kids he was aware of the monster rumor. He said that a developer started spreading it and the neighborhood bully is his nephew.

1(Randy)

They've been after my manor for a long time. They were trying to run me out so they can buy it and remodel it into their new headquarters.

2(Axton}

Sounds like they will stop at nothing, until they get this place.

3(Chris)

Hmm. There may be a way to put a stop to this.

4(Ashlei)

I sure hope this plan is better than your last one.

The kids told their parents what the bully has been doing. Their folks told the whole neighborhood. They all told the bully to go into the manor and get the kids' stuff back. Just as he opened the door, he heard snarling and saw eyes shining in the dark. The bully began to stutter and said, "You don't scare me! I float like a bee and sting like a butterfly." The kids burst out laughing, because they couldn't believe he was really terrified, and he had that saying backwards.

Brodie came out and snarled at the bully. The kids told everyone in the neighborhood that Brodie, the rottweiler, was the monster they all saw. Randy explained everything to the neighborhood, then made the bully give back all the kids' stuff he threw. After that, the bully and his uncle were forced to clean up around the manor for punishment.

A few days later, Randy was having a party at his manor. He invited the whole neighborhood over, including the kids. They arrived and saw Randy and Brodie, then walked to them. Randy thanked the kids for saving his home. Music began to play, and then everyone in the dining room started dancing. So did the Kids.

1(Ashlei)

Come on, Axton! Let's dance.

2(Axton)

Oh, boy. Then again, why not?

3(Chris)

Hey, Brodie. Come join the party!

Everyone was having fun dancing, and even Brodie joined in. Thanks to the kids the bully and his uncle paid for the mess they caused, saved Randy from losing his home, all the kids in the neighborhood got all their stuff back, and they revealed who and what the monster in the manor really was.

THE END!

Made in the USA
Middletown, DE
20 July 2022

69621226R00020